Teddy Ruxpin's Christmas

This story shows the value of gathering together
with friends at Christmastime.

Story by:
Will Ryan

Illustrated by:

Russell Hicks   Lorann Downer
Douglas McCarthy   Rivka
Allyn Conley-Gorniak   Matthew Bates
Julie Ann Armstrong   Fay Whitemountain

WORLDS OF WONDER™

Worlds of Wonder, Inc. is the exclusive licensee, manufacturer and distributor of The World of Teddy Ruxpin toys.
"The World of Teddy Ruxpin" and "Teddy Ruxpin" are trademarks of Alchemy II, Inc., Chatsworth, CA.
The symbol **W•W** and "Worlds of Wonder" are trademarks of Worlds of Wonder, Inc., Fremont, California.

Grubby™   Newton Gimmick™   Princess Aruzia™   Leota™   Wooly What's-It™

Prince Arin™   Fobs®

Teddy

Hi, there! I'm Teddy Ruxpin.

Grubby

And Grubby, everybody! I'm Merry Christmas!

Teddy

What?!

Grubby

Aw, I mean Merry Christmas, everybody! I'm Grubby.

Teddy

Grubby and I know that where you live, Christmas is just about the best holiday of the year.

Grubby

Yup.

Teddy

And since we like to share our Grundo holidays with you, we thought it would be nice to help you celebrate the joy of Christmas.

Grubby

And what better way to spread Christmas cheer than to sing about it!

Page 1

"Here We Come A-Caroling"

Here we come a-caroling among the
  leaves so green.
Here we come a-wandering, so fair
  to be seen.

Love and joy come to you
And to you, your Wassail, too.
And God bless you and send you a
	happy new year.
And God send you a happy new year.

"Deck The Halls"

Deck the halls with boughs of holly,
Fa la la la la la la la la.
'Tis the season to be jolly,
Fa la la la la la la la la.

Don we now our gay apparel,
Fa la la la la la la la la.
Troll the ancient Yuletide carol,
Fa la la la la la la la la,
Fa la la la la la la la la.

"Good King Wenceslas"

Good King Wenceslas looked out
On the Feast of Stephen.
When the snow lay round about,
Deep and crisp and even.
Brightly shone the moon that night,
Though the frost was cruel.
When a poor man came in sight,
Gathering winter fuel.

"The Holly and The Ivy"

The holly and the ivy
When they are both full grown,
Of all the trees that are in the wood,
The holly bears the crown.
The rising of the sun,
And the running of the deer,
The playing of the merry organ,
Sweet singing in the choir.

Grubby
Hey, Teddy! Here come some of our friends a-carolin'!

Teddy
Hello, Gimmick! Would it be okay to join you?

Gimmick
Hello, boys!

Gimmick
Oh, by all means!

All

Love and joy come to you,
And to you, your Wassail, too.
And God bless you and send you a
   happy new year.
And God send you a happy new year.
Happy new year.

Grubby

That was fun, Teddy.

Teddy

It sure was.

Gimmick

Precisely!

Teddy

Hey, everybody, now that we're all together, can we sing our special Grundo version of "The Twelve Days of Christmas"?

All

Yea! Oh, boy! Mi, mi, mi, mi, mi!
How wonderful!

Gimmick

Here we go!

"The Twelve Days of Christmas"
(Grundo Version)

On the first day of Christmas,
Grubby gave to me
Wooly in a Boggleberry Tree.

On the second day of Christmas,
Teddy gave to me
Two Anythings.

On the third day of Christmas,
L.B. gave to me
Three cannonballs.

On the fourth day of Christmas,
Teddy gave to me
Four pairs of socks.

On the fifth day of Christmas,
Grubby gave to me
Five roasted roots.

On the sixth day of Christmas,
Teddy gave to us
Six magic Crystals.

On the seventh day of Christmas,
Leota gave to me
Seven sprites a-flying.

On the eighth day of Christmas,
Wooly What's-It gave to me
Eight Fobs a-singing.

On the ninth day of Christmas
A Mudblup gave to me
Nine Grunges strumming.

On the tenth day of Christmas,
Aruzia gave to me
Ten Gutangs a-marching.

On the eleventh day of Christmas,
Grubby gave to me
Eleven Wogglies leaping.

On the twelfth day of Christmas,
We'd like to give to you
Twelve Bounders bounding.

Grubby

That sure is a complicated song, Teddy.

Teddy

It is?

Grubby

Yup. Why I ran outta' legs just tryin' to keep tracka' all those days.

Gimmick

Well, Grubby, here's a medley of familiar songs that just might ring a bell with you.

Grubby

Oh, boy!

"Hark, How The Bells"

Hark, how the bells, sweet silver bells,
All seem to say, throw cares away.
Christmas is here, bringing good cheer
To young and old, meek and the bold.
Ding dong ding dong, that is their song
With joyful ring, all caroling.
One seems to hear words of good cheer
From everywhere, filling the air.
Oh, how they pound, raising the sound,
O'er hill and dale, telling their tale.

Gaily they ring while people sing
Songs of good cheer. Christmas is here.
Merry, merry, merry, merry Christmas.
Merry, merry, merry, merry Christmas.
On, on they send, on without end,
Their joyful tone to every home.

Teddy

Gee, that was pretty.

Grubby

Yeah, let's sing it again.

"Jingle Bells"

Dashing through the snow
In a one-horse open sleigh.
O'er the fields we go
Laughing all the way.
Bells on Bobtail ring
Making spirits bright.
What fun it is to ride and sing
A sleighing song tonight.

Chorus

Jingle bells, jingle bells,
Jingle all the way!
Oh, what fun it is to ride
In a one-horse open sleigh!
Jingle bells, jingle bells,
Jingle all the way!
Oh, what fun it is to ride
In a one-horse open sleigh!

Repeat Chorus

Teddy

That sounded really nice, everybody.

Grubby

Yeah, but it musta' been too loud.

Gimmick

Why do you say that, Grubby?

Grubby

'Cause my ears are still ringin'.

Teddy

Hey, look! Here come some more carolers.

Grubby

Let's join 'em, Teddy.

Teddy

Okay, Grubby.

"Oh, Christmas Tree"

Oh, Christmas tree,
Oh, Christmas tree,
How lovely are thy branches.
Oh, Christmas tree,
Oh, Christmas tree,
How lovely are thy branches.
To every girl and every boy,
It speaks of holidays and joy.
Oh, Christmas tree,
Oh, Christmas tree,
How lovely are thy branches.

Gimmick

I've got a great idea, Teddy. Why don't you and Grubby tell us the story of "The Night Before Christmas"?

Teddy

Okay, Gimmick.

Grubby

Oh, boy!

"The Night Before Christmas"

'Twas the night before Christmas, and all through the house
Not a creature was stirring, not even a mouse.
All the stockings were hung by the chimney with care,
In hopes that Saint Nicholas soon would be there.
Mama in her kerchief and I in my cap
Had just settled down for a long winter's nap.

When out on the lawn there arose such a clatter,
I sprang from my bed to see what was the matter.
Away to the window I flew like a flash.
Tore open the shutters, and threw up the sash.
The moon on the breast of the new fallen snow,
Gave a luster of midday to objects below.
When what to my wonderin' eyes should appear,
But a miniature sleigh and eight tiny reindeer.

With a little old driver so lively and quick.
I knew in a moment who it was, Saint Nick.
More rapid than eagles, his coursers they came,
And he whistled and shouted and called them by name,
"Now Dasher, now Dancer, now Prancer, now Vixen,
On Comet, on Cupid, on Donner, on Blitzen,
To the top of the porch, to the top of the wall,
Now dash away, dash away all!"
So, up to the house top the coursers they flew,

With the sleigh full of toys and Saint Nicholas, too.
And then in a twinkling I heard on the roof
The prancing and pawing of each little hoof.
As I drew in my head and was turning around,
Down the chimney he came with a bound.
He was dressed all in fur from his head to his foot.
And his clothes were all tarnished with ashes and soot.
A bundle of toys he had flung on his back,
And he looked like a peddler just opening his pack.

His eyes, how they twinkled, his dimples, how merry,
His cheeks were like roses, his nose, like a cherry.
His droll little mouth was drawn up like a bow,
And the beard on his chin was as white as the snow.
The stump of a pipe he held tight in his teeth,
And the smoke, it encircled his head like a wreath.
He had a broad face and a round little belly,
That shook when he laughed, like a bowl full of jelly.
He was chubby and plump, a right jolly old elf.
And I laughed when I saw him, in spite of myself.

A wink of his eye, and a twist of his head,
Soon gave me to know I had nothing to dread.
He spoke not a word but went straight to his work,
And filled all the stockings, then turned with a jerk.
And laying a finger aside of his nose,
And giving a nod up the chimney he rose.
He sprang to his sleigh, to his team gave a whistle.
And away they all flew like the down of a thistle.
But I heard him exclaim as he drove out of sight,
"Merry Christmas to all, and to all good night."

"We Wish You A Merry Christmas"

We wish you a merry Christmas.
We wish you a merry Christmas.
We wish you a merry Christmas,
And a happy new year.
Good tidings we bring
To you and your kin,
Good tidings for Christmas
And a happy new year.
We wish you a merry Christmas.
We wish you a merry Christmas.
We wish you a merry Christmas,
And a happy new year.

Teddy
Merry Christmas, everybody!